The Fish House Door

Yellow

Astrid Sheckels
2010

Published by

Islandport Press

P.O. Box 10

267 U.S. Route One, Suite B

Yarmouth, Maine 04096

www.islandportpress.com

ISBN: 978-1-934031-30-8

Library of Congress Control Number: 2010925773

Printed in China

ISLANDPORT PRESS · YARMOUTH · MAINE

Dedicated to Rev. Bobby Ives, a great Maine storyteller
who showed me the real fish house door

—ROBERT F. BALDWIN

For Oliver and the people of Frenchboro, Maine

—ASTRID SHECKELS

"I listened to the waves lapping the rocks under the dock. The bright colors of the door sparkled in the sunlight. I couldn't take my eyes off it. Every smear of red, white, yellow, and brown looked like it belonged just where it was. It really was a masterpiece."

The Fish House Door

Robert F. Baldwin   Astrid Sheckels

I was steering my dad's lobster boat up the channel while Dad leaned back against the pilot house after a morning of hard work. As we idled through the harbor, I saw someone standing on our dock. I couldn't tell who it was, but from the way he stared at the door of our fish house, I guessed he must be a new summer person.

He greeted us on the wharf. He was wearing clean, faded jeans and a sweatshirt, and said his name was Mr. Bruckner. He wanted to buy a couple of lobsters.

"What size?" Dad asked.

"Big enough for two hungry summer people," Mr. Bruckner said. He didn't ask the price.

I climbed down to the float, hauled a crate of lobsters from the water, and grabbed a pair that looked about a pound and a half each. They thrashed about, waving their banded claws and snapping their wet tails.

"Fifteen dollars," Dad said. "Got something to carry them in?"

The man shook his head.

"Good thing you don't want more than two," Dad said.

With a lobster in each hand, Mr. Bruckner walked up the path toward the main road. Before he'd gone fifty yards he turned and waved a lobster in the direction of our fish house.

"I like that door," he said.

"Ayuh," Dad called back. "It's a good door."

I looked at the paint-smeared door, blazing red and yellow in the afternoon sun. Why, I thought, would a rich summer person say he liked that beat-up old door? The door was a mess. Whenever Dad or I painted our trap buoys or repainted the skiff, we cleaned our paintbrushes against it. I kind of liked it though, the same way I liked the stink of old bait bags and how the harbor smelled at low tide. They all reminded me of our island. What I couldn't figure out was why a stranger would like it.

When we got up to the house, I handed Mom the mail we'd picked up at the post office.

"Met a new summer person," Dad told her. She didn't say anything and continued opening the mail. "He told me he really likes the fish house door." She glanced up and raised an eyebrow.

"Well, shoot, Anne, that's not so strange," Dad said. "I kind of like it myself. And by the way he pays top dollar for lobster."

"He better buy a lot of it then," she replied. "The bills just keep coming and coming."

I've never really known if my family is rich or poor or somewhere in the middle. Once when I was younger, my older sister, Helen, said we were poor, but I'm not so sure. Dad says we have everything we need, including a house and dock that plenty of millionaires would love to own. But we do seem to have a lot of bills.

By the time I went down to the wharf the next morning, the sun was already peeking over the trees, and there wasn't enough breeze to stir the tops of the spruce trees surrounding the harbor. Most island men were already out hauling traps. The sounds of their engines floated across the smooth water and into the harbor. A few others were at the island lobster pound getting ready. We'd hauled most of our traps the day before so Dad decided he'd give the lobsters another day to find our bait.

Dad was sitting on a crate, surrounded by freshly painted yellow and red trap buoys. Every lobsterman paints his buoys a specific color and pattern, so they can tell who owns each and every buoy. There were some old wooden buoys lying around that Dad sold to tourists, as well as some broken traps in need of repair, and small coils of rope measured out in fathoms. The air was dry and smelled of spruce and the ocean. I got a brush and started helping him paint. I was painting the next to the last buoy when Mr. Bruckner stopped by again, this time carrying a bucket.

"Be right with you," Dad said. Mr. Bruckner stood off to one side and watched as we dipped the tips of our brushes into the red paint and carefully cut in along the edge of the yellow. When we were done, Dad handed me his brush. I stepped over to the fish house and wiped the wet brushes back and forth against the door, transferring the paint from bristle to board. When I turned, I saw Mr. Bruckner staring at the door with his head cocked slightly to one side.

"You an artist?" Dad asked.

He grinned. "What makes you think that?"

Dad didn't say anything.

"No, I'm not an artist," Mr. Bruckner continued. "I'm an art dealer. I own a gallery."

"I don't know much about art," Dad said, "but I guess Shawn and I have done a bit of painting in our time. Huh, Shawn?"

I nodded.

"You'd be surprised how many summer people buy lobster buoys, especially the old wooden ones," Dad told him. "How about a couple for your gallery? Better yet, how about a hand-painted fish house door?" He laughed.

Mr. Bruckner looked again at the door. "No, thanks. Just some lobsters will do today," he said.

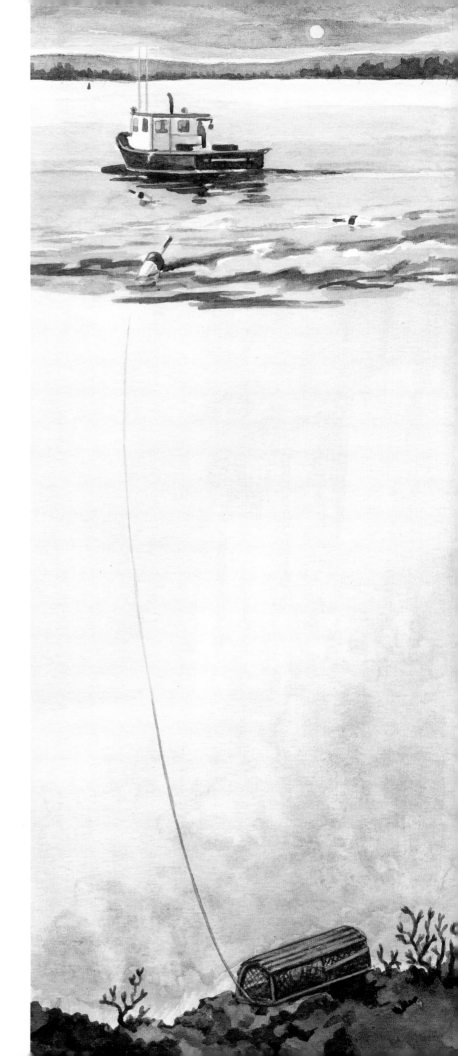

After he walked away, I looked at the door, thinking how great it would be if an art dealer would really pay money for our old fish house door. I was doubtful, but Dad was a great salesman.

He would have to be. Like the rest of the old fish house, the door had seen better days. It was loose in the joints, and the screws had pulled out of some of the hinges. It didn't close tightly any more, and we latched it with a short piece of rope.

The front of the door was smeared with years and years of paint, mostly yellow and red now, of course, but I could still see traces of blue and white.

"Those were your grandfather's colors," Dad said. "I can remember the first time I hauled one of his blue and white buoys out of the bay.

"It was my tenth birthday, the day Pa decided I was old enough to do man's work. The sky had just begun to get light when we dropped our mooring and motored out. The moon was setting. The air was chilly and damp. I was shivering, but I felt proud that I was finally going out to haul traps.

"Back then," he continued, "we used wooden traps and the harbor was lined with fish houses and working docks. When I wasn't hauling traps, I was baiting pockets for the older fishermen, or helping repair traps in this fish house with your Grampa Dick and Uncle John."

"The door must have looked different in those days," I said.

"It was blue and white, mostly, with a lot more weathered boards showing between the paint streaks. You could still see traces of brown."

Dad told me that brown and white had been the colors of Grampa Alec's trap buoys, which were carved out of wood. Now, they're made of foam. Grampa Alec was actually my great-grandfather, but I never met him.

"What was he like?" I asked.

"Well, he wasn't great at fishing or lobstering, but he was a terrific boatbuilder and carpenter."

Dad said there were thirty-two or so families living on the island year-round when Grampa Alec built the fish house. There was even a year-round store. Nearly all the men fished, but Grampa spent as much time building dories as fishing.

"He didn't get paid much for them," Dad said, "but there was a time when most island men fished from boats built by your great-grandfather and, before that, his father.

"In the summers, the passenger ferry used to visit twice a week, but during the winter, people had to use their own boats to get to the mainland. We didn't have any telephones or electricity, either. When the weather was bad, we were cut off from the rest of the world.

"During winter storms, I used to crawl into Grampa Alec's lap in the chair next to the woodstove. While the bay exploded against the icy rocks and the tide surged down the harbor, he'd smoke his pipe and tell me about trips on the coasting schooners that sailed all the way to Portland, and Boston, and Baltimore.

"I really loved that man. When I was eight, we moved off the island to go to the mainland school. One day, his boat caught fire off Parson's Ledge. They never found him."

"What did he look like?"

"What I remember were his thick, calloused hands and the color of his eyes. They were brown. Just like his trap buoys."

Every summer, Dad and his family returned to the island, just like our family does. He hauled traps with his father until it was time to go back to school. Just like I do. Someday, I'll have my own lobster boat, too.

Mr. Bruckner was renting the old Morris house for the whole summer, and we saw him two or three times a week. He would come by with his bucket to buy lobsters, sometimes just a couple for his wife and himself, sometimes a bunch for his guests. He often looked at the fish house door, and even took some pictures of it, but he didn't really mention it again.

Then one day toward the end of August, just before he was going to leave, Mr. Bruckner asked if he could go out with us on the boat to haul traps. "I suppose so," Dad said, "as long as you're willing to stay out there until I'm done."

Actually, he was pretty useful. He even baited some pockets, and he didn't get seasick, either. On the way home I started thinking again about the fish house door. Before I took off my boots I deliberately stopped in front of the fish house and studied it the way Mr. Bruckner had done the first day I'd met him. I pretended I was admiring a famous painting to see what he would say.

"Ah, yes," Mr. Bruckner said. "The fish house door masterpiece."

I looked at him to see if he was trying to be funny. He wasn't smiling. He had that look that summer people get when they want something. Dad must have noticed it too because he walked over and began admiring the door with me.

"You still like that door?" Dad asked.

"Still do," Mr. Bruckner said. "I like the improbable combination of colors and textures."

Dad didn't say anything.

"Look at the way the weathered wood shows through where the paint has peeled off—and the little flecks of old colors. And look over here," he said, pointing to a bare patch of wood where Grampa Alec had once sketched a boat design. "It looks like some old boatbuilder once used this part of the door as a drawing board. And over here someone added up a column of numbers, maybe selling lobsters to summer people."

Mr. Bruckner sounded like he was the one trying to sell the door. "You can't plan that kind of beauty," he said. "It just happens, artlessly. It's a simple work, created by simple fishermen. And it happens to be magnificent."

Maybe Mr. Bruckner didn't know much after all. The door was just a door, and Dad was about to sell it for way more than any "simple fisherman" would pay.

"Would you take five hundred dollars for it?" Mr. Bruckner asked. *Five hundred dollars!* I thought. *Yes!* I turned away to hide my smile as I ran my hand across the streaks of dried paint.

Dad lifted his cap and ran his fingers through his hair.

"One thousand?" Mr. Bruckner asked, but this time I barely heard him. I had noticed something on the door. A tiny patch of brown paint, almost covered up by the newer, brighter colors. As I stared at it, I imagined the eyes of my great-grandfather. I could picture him telling stories at the wharf and imagined the smell of woodsmoke and pipe tobacco and the roar of winter surf.

Dad stepped a little closer to see what I was staring at, and he saw the brown paint, too. "Okay," Mr. Bruckner said, "make it two thousand."

I listened to the waves lapping the rocks under the dock. The bright colors of the door sparkled in the sunlight. I couldn't take my eyes off it. Every smear of red, white, yellow, and brown looked like it belonged just where it was. It really was a masterpiece.

"Sorry," Dad said.

Mr. Bruckner shook his head. "It's an excellent price."

Dad was silent, but I knew what he was thinking.

"Mr. Bruckner," I said, "that might be a good price for a simple piece of art, but this is my family's fish house door. We wouldn't sell it for a million dollars. Now, would you like any lobsters to take home with you?"

ROBERT F. BALDWIN

Robert F. Baldwin (1934–2007) was a modern-day troubadour, singing, playing the banjo, and collecting and telling stories wherever he went. His articles and stories have appeared in *Sea Frontiers, Down East, Offshore, Maine Boats, Homes and Harbors,* and *Yankee.* His children's books include *New England Whaler, This Is the Sea that Feeds Us,* and *Cities Through Time: Beijing.* After living in Virginia, North Carolina, Massachusetts, Rhode Island, and Iowa, Bob and his wife Annabelle settled in Newcastle, Maine, where Bob first heard the story of the fish house door.

ASTRID SHECKELS

Astrid Sheckels was born and raised in the farming town of Hatfield, Massachusetts. She cannot remember a time when she wasn't listening to, telling, or illustrating stories. Her detailed illustrations give every story more depth and dimension, and the scenes and faces in *The Fish House Door* are based on location photo shoots with real New Englanders. Astrid's first children's book, *The Scallop Christmas,* written by Jane Freeberg and published by Islandport Press, won a 2009 Maine Lupine Honor Award, given annually to a picture book of outstanding merit. She lives, paints, and teaches in western Massachusetts.